Under the

Baobab Tree

Pratibha N. Reebye

Note for Librarians: A cataloguing record for this book is available from Library and Archives Canada at www.collectionscanada.ca/amicus/index-e.html
ISBN 1-4120-9142-x

Printed on paper with minimum 30% recycled fibre.
Trafford's print shop runs on "green energy" from solar, wind and other environmentally-friendly power sources.

PUBLISHING™
Offices in Canada, USA, Ireland and UK

Book sales for North America and international:
Trafford Publishing, 6E–2333 Government St.,
Victoria, BC V8T 4P4 CANADA
phone 250 383 6864 (toll-free 1 888 232 4444)
fax 250 383 6804; email to orders@trafford.com
Book sales in Europe:
Trafford Publishing (UK) Limited, 9 Park End Street, 2nd Floor
Oxford, UK OX1 1HH UNITED KINGDOM
phone 44 (0)1865 722 113 (local rate 0845 230 9601)
facsimile 44 (0)1865 722 868; info.uk@trafford.com
Order online at:
trafford.com/06-0896

10 9 8 7 6 5 4 3 2

To my mother.

*Who exemplifies reason to celebrate nothingness,
and taught us the immense value of patience.*

Preface

Someone once asked me, "Why do you have to write?"

I looked at him in disbelief. Do you have to have a reason to write? Maybe, he meant that there is no need to publish. I gave the whole process a little bit of thought. For the past ten years or more, I have always expressed myself through words, written or spoken. Prior to that, the urge to write was not strong. It was very important for me to express myself through drawings, paintings, collections of art pieces.

Something happened to me two years ago. A great void which can only be filled by words. Nothing else mattered. I thought everyone kind of did that by writing diaries, chronicles. This urge, however, was stronger, and addictive. The more I wrote, the more I wanted to express on paper. This insatiable urge would be calmed only if I had an audience. My family will not be good pinnacles. I do not want to reach them. They share many of the experiences of which I have written, and are at the heart of some of the stories. In others, they may not be interested.

Yes, I do have a specific purpose. It is to reach persons who will never see my kind of world, or the world that only myself and persons like me can appreciate. These stories are written for those who do not look like me, or have not had childhood experiences like me, or opportunities to negotiate two or three worlds, all at once.

You guessed correctly; I am trying to portray the immigrant's world. These are stories based on true experiences. I cannot take credit for all of those experiences. I was fortunate in experiencing some, and sad that some experiences left me with unnecessary trauma.... However, the majority of my contributions have come from strangers. These are not stories about racism, and these are not my attempts to alter the world. I want to create, simply, human emotional characters. I want to stir the feelings, I want the profile of an immigrant man or woman or child to fizz.

There is no such thing as an immigrant or a displaced person. I invite you to look at these characters with your inner eye. These characters are so commonplace that you may have encountered them somewhere, somehow. If not, seek them.

Growing Up

Today, Thakur Lal's house looked different. The verandah was scrubbed with soap and water, with some eucalyptus branches added to the water for fragrance. The wooden floor then was smeared generously with turtle wax specially meant for the oak floor. And that was not all. Sudha, the maid, had been brushing the floor with a coconut brush for at least 45 minutes. The result? The fifty-five-year-old oak floor was able to reflect the shadows of the bougainvillea twigs and join their dance to the tunes of a quiet, gentle, silky breeze.

There was no one around. *Everything looks different*, thought Hari. All the window panes shone in their weather-beaten wooden frames. There were fresh-cut flowers— yellow zinnias in tall brass vases. It was difficult to decide if the brass shone more because of the borrowed gold from the zinnias, or if the sunrays were making the special effects. The big portrait of Hari's grandfather was actually aligned! As far as Hari could remember, this portrait always seemed crooked. It was hung quite low over the door frame, and tall persons invariably inadvertently knocked their heads on it. Hari and his favourite cousin Binda had devised a game around this portrait. If grandpa's bushy moustache was tilted to the right they would have a good day. If not, they would have some trouble at home or school. Hari had devised an antidote for this calamity. If he turned himself around three times and did not walk on the cracks between the stone slabs of the road leading to school, usually nothing happened. Binda did not like this idea. Hari always felt that girls thought differently from boys, and bore no offence to her.

So what is going on? thought Hari. He had started to lose patience. He would have expected the house to look that clean during Diwali festival. He knew that everything had to be clean during Diwali, even the children! Hari scanned the verandah with his sharp brown eyes. The only imperfections Hari could see were the straight spears of sunrays allowing dust particles to ride on them, making funny designs. Well, Hari had to solve this mystery of the house, so clean that it almost felt like Diwali time.

He decided he wanted to whistle. The first time when he tried, no sound came. He got really edgy. After practising for a whole hour, no sound? Even Raja and Baban were whistling tunes. Maybe he should try to put two fingers in his mouth and whistle. But then Mom and Nani would hear him, that is, if he succeeded in that method. He knew that his grandma would be very upset, as she thought whistling would bring bad luck. Suddenly, he felt terribly alone, and hungry!

"Mom, where are you? I am hungry, Mom."

"Oh Ram, Ram! Why did you enter from the verandah? Did you not know we are expecting guests? Sudha will get really mad at you; look at the mud —"

"No, Mom, I haven't touched anything—look, I have my

chappals* in my hands and I am walking on my tippy toes!" Hari made his way from a side door that went to the outside porch, leading to their kitchen.

The kitchen was a kind of stone hut with a tin roof. Behind the outdoor kitchen was a tall avocado tree loaded with greenish purple fruit, and two pawpaw trees. In contrast to the heavy look of the mature avocado tree, the papaya tree looked like a tall lanky teenager, quite unsure of himself.

The eastern wall was completely covered by passion fruit climbers. One could not see the hidden fruit that well, because last week's rain had given permission for many young leaves to appear, and they seemed to have occupied every square inch of this wall. The biggest attraction of the kitchen, however, lay in the authentic outdoor stove which was constantly kept going with wooden twigs collected from a nearby patch of forest. The kitchen and stove seemed terribly busy. Hari recognised the aroma of fried jamuns† and puris‡.

And he suddenly remembered—today was D-day. How could he forget an important event such as this? He had overheard a conversation between his mom and his grandma, about "someone coming to see Didi§ to marry her…Tell Radha to wear that blue silk saree, and she can wear my gold bangles and…."

"Hari, what are you looking at? Wash your face, change your uniform and go and sit on the temple wall. As soon as you

---

* chappals: slippers
† jamuns: fried Indian sweets
‡ puris: fried wheat bread
§ didi: older sister

see them coming, tell me."

Suddenly, Hari felt very important. He, an eight-year-old, who had no standing at all in the household full of children—he would be the first one to see these important guests! His first impulse was to ask Binda, the favourite cousin, to accompany him. After a quick review, he decided against this. It was his responsibility and he was going to accomplish it single-handedly.

His heart filled with pride, he walked towards the temple. The temple was a small concrete building at the outer wall surrounding their land. It was quite a ways from the kitchen. In fact, it was difficult to see it from that angle. As the main house was build on elevated ground, its bouquets of alternating red and orange bougainvilleas could be seen from the temple. The temple had all the Hindu gods guarding Thakur Lal's property. Hari's favourite god was Lord Hanuman*, who supposedly was so strong that he could lift mountains on the tip of his little finger. Hari had a secret wish to obtain power from Lord Hanuman.

He now stationed himself on the wall, his legs dangling. He could scan the road quite easily from there. He almost felt like a warrior guarding his castle. Ten minutes passed. Nothing changed. Only two stray dogs walked past him. One of them begged with his paws lifted. Reluctantly, Hari shared with the dog some pieces from his snack of puris. But the dog wanted more. Ultimately, Hari lost his patience. He aimed a stone at the dog. No sooner had he done that when he noticed Babulal's taxi which was heading their way. With its rickety doors and coughing sounds, it was difficult to ignore. And Hari was on duty anyway.

---

* Hanuman: powerful deity with monkey body

So they have taken a taxi rather than a tonga*; they must be rich, thought Hari. He had never been in a taxi before. He had heard that it cost at least 50 rupees† from the railway station. Hari wanted to alert his mom but he also wanted to see who was inside this taxi.

There were seven persons in a small taxi meant for four. Hari counted again: an old man with a pugri‡ in the front, a small girl on his lap who seemed to be sucking a lollipop; on the backseat, there were two men and two women. Which one was going to be Didi's husband? *Not the one with the glasses, I hope.* And the other one had a cigarette in his mouth. Which one?

He had to hurry now. He jumped and made a beehive for the kitchen. "Mom, Mom, they are here." he was panting but he had accomplished his mission successfully.

His mom wiped his face with her saree. That was her way of showing her appreciation. He knew that well. Now all the children were told to disappear. His duty was over. No one cared about him now. Suddenly, Hari felt sad, very sad. His mom, grandma, even uncles and dad were all gathered on the verandah. Where was Didi?

Other children in the Thakur household had started gathering around him. He was being bombarded with questions. Did he really see Didi's bridegroom-to-be? Did any children come with him? Did they talk to him?.......... Hari now climbed onto the second wave of exaltation. He was again an important person not to be ignored. This time his audience constituted

---

* tonga: a horse cart
† rupee: Indian currency
‡ pugri: a turban or cloth hat, usually coloured

Sheela, age two-and-a-half years, through to Binda who was the same age as he, with three other cousins in between in age.

This feeling of importance did not last long. Binda seemed to know about what was going on in much more detail than he. He was shaken when Binda in her typical nasal voice blurted out, "If they like your Didi, she will be married during the summer holidays. My pa told me that we will visit her in her new home," and, "You know that man with the cigarette is the one. The other one is his friend."

What am I hearing? Hari thought. Although as a rule he never believed what Binda told him, today she seemed to be talking with conviction. *My Didi, go away? And that too with a man smoking a cigarette? And on top of everything, taking her away from me?*

He felt like a deflated balloon. His head hurt. He wanted to cry and hit these men!

You cannot come here and steal my sister. Wait till I teach you a lesson! The anger poured from his eyes. He could not listen to Binda's requests not to enter the verandah. He shoved her aside and darted to where this drama was actually taking place.

Then he saw the look in his Didi's eyes. She was looking at this man who had the cigarette in his mouth with so much love. The gentleman seemed to be captivated by her as well.

Ugh! So Didi likes him too! What am I to do?

"Come here, Beta. What beautiful eyes he has got, the strange lady was saying. The girl sucking the lollipop had become very sticky all over and now another duty was bestowed on him.

"Hari, take her inside and find someone to wash her hands."

Wash her hands? Yuck. Before he could make an excuse and escape from this "brat," he overheard the strange lady saying, "He seems so gentle, so smart yet polite. You are so lucky to have a responsible son like him. Otherwise, the children these days…"

Hari had no need for further comments. He again was feeling like a well-inflated balloon, wanting to explore the skies!

He was polite, responsible, trustworthy. With a little bit of help from Lord Hanuman, he may even be able to tolerate separation from his beloved Didi….

And it happened!

He actually whistled. The whistle was loud, happy, as if singing about his promotion from a child who could do nothing right to a young man who had beautiful brown eyes, who was polite.

He whistled again, strongly and happily!!

ദ

Transformation

On a humid summer afternoon at the Toronto airport three silhouettes were visible through the semitransparent glass panes. One was that of a slim female with long blonde hair, the other of a gentleman with a prominent forehead, and the third silhouette was of a small child who sat slouched in the chair. It was actually a foursome, but the baby was sitting on the woman's lap and would not have been visible from outside.

The little boy was myself, Enrique, age two years and nine months. My baby brother was almost five months old then. I would not have had any recollections about that day when we entered Canada if it were not for my mom, who kept an album and diary of events. My father's friend, who was waiting with balloons, teddy bears and flowers to greet us, took this picture showing three of us in the immigration department. I am a ten-year-old now. Time truly has flown!

"Enrique, what is the magic word?"
"Yes, mother. I mean, please, mother."
"You must excuse my poor darling, Ms Fraser. He has just started learning his English, and as for his manners..."

The rest of the conversation was muffled, but I knew what

was being said. The conversation with my piano teacher Ms Fraser must have been about how these poor darlings were left in a crowded Brazilian orphanage. How my mom had to bribe the nurse, attendant and a social worker to get access to this most beautiful boy with the saddest eyes! Also, an account of how the orphanage administration twisted their arms and forced them to adopt my half-brother Sebastian as well.

On some other occasions, I remembered how my dad talked about my body size.

"When we saw him at first, we thought he was a one- year-old rather than two- and-a- half years old," Dad used to say.

The first night in my adopted parents' suburban house was very frightening. I was gently tucked in my bed. My baby brother slept in my parents' room. In the middle of the night I woke up and was frightened by the big teddy bear which was placed at the foot of my bed.

"Dora, Dora!" I remember screaming.

Dora was the nurse attached to our wing of the orphanage. She was a middle-aged Brazilian woman who took great pride in looking after the children in her wing with few resources. She must have liked me, because I was the chosen one to sit on her lap out of 14 wailing children ranging from two to four years. Now Dora did not come, but my dad was there. He placed his hand on my racing heart, gave me a gentle hug and said, "Shhhh, everything will be okay. Try to sleep."

He was right. Nights became easier to handle.

"I want to sit on your lap, Mom. Why is it always

Sebastian?" I was seven now, and questioning my mother.

"You are the big boy, you should know how to behave," Mom replied.

"Leave him alone, Marg. Come on, silly boy, sit on my lap if you want to." My dad was compromising.

"No, No, No! I want mommy and no one else."

"Okay then, go, and call your mom from Brazil," retorted my frustrated mother.

"Shhh, what are you saying, Marg? Enrique, go to your room." Dad was now clearly upset.

My closet knows about my tears, kicks, and trashing episodes. Who was this "my mom" from Brazil? Why did she leave me? Why is mom telling me lies?

After what seemed an eternity, dad and mom both entered my room, telling me how sorry they were for hurting my feelings. But they did not tell me that I did not have a Brazilian mother!

Sebastian has always been a smart boy. He knew his colors and alphabet from age three, when I was still struggling with my numbers and alphabet at age seven! I also had an "image" problem. I did not like my black eyes, my dark hair, and above all my name, Enrique. Sebastian did not care for outward appearance and became a true Canadian very quickly.

Why am I so different? What is wrong with me?

Last month, an interesting thing happened in our class. A boy of my age entered our school in the middle of the term. His name was Diego, and he could not speak English at all. Our teachers told us he was from Brazil and we were all supposed to help him with his English. His name sounded weirder than mine did. I'd already taught my friends to call me Dean, which was my adoptive father's middle name.

In the gym class, a bully tried to trip Diego with his feet when the teacher was not looking, but I spotted him and saved Diego from falling. Diego's profuse thanks in Spanish sounded sweet to my ears and I vowed to help him from then onwards.

Diego and I are becoming inseparable. Our gym teacher even stated that we could pass as real brothers. One day, my mother came to fetch Sebastian and me from school. I was playing with Diego on the school grounds with Sebastian watching us.

"Enrique, what are you doing? Come quickly inside the car," my mom was saying. Sebastian had already entered the car.

"Mom, can we give Diego a ride?" I pleaded with my mom.

"Of course not," mom retorted. "His parents may not like that. And he should be returning home. There are hardly any children on the playground."

"Adios, bye, Dean." Diego tried his half-Spanish, half-English with me.

"What is he saying? I do not want your friend to use that name, is that clear? Otherwise, I will not like you to play with him."

"Why not? He is from Brazil and you told me I had a Brazilian mom too." It was an inopportune remark, which always made my mom sad or angry.

Today, mom was neither angry nor sad. She seemed determined.

"Do not tease me more. You want to know about your Brazilian mother? If it's so important, then I will tell you." Out came the famous album, and yellowed documents, and files neatly labeled Sebastian, and Enrique.

My mom then told me I was to read these documents when I turned sixteen. For the time being, she told me my birthmother was a Brazilian woman who was called Maria. She did not know her last name. She used to sell candles on the road, and sometimes beg for food when she was hungry.

My mom was told Maria was very thin and became sick, so she decided to leave me in the orphanage. With the birth of Sebastian, Maria probably was very sick and died, but no one was sure. The convent nuns who ran the orphanage took responsibility for the newborn. Thus, Sebastian did not know our birth mom at all.

"Did she cry when she left me in the orphanage?"

At my question, my mom started crying, holding me tight. "I do not know for sure, but her heart must have been broken to leave a beautiful boy like you in the orphanage."

Mom's tears were contagious. Soon, Sebastian joined us in our emotional sobbing.

"You know, there was one thing Maria requested, and we always tried to respect it. She never wanted your names to be changed in case you were adopted. That is why I was angry when Diego called you by another name. It was the only thing she could give you before she left."

Here I was, hardly ten years old, and now knew for sure that the persons whom I called Mom and Dad were definitely not my birthparents. I tried to pretend with my classmates that I was

Dean, not Enrique. Being Enrique meant living inside the body of a Brazilian orphan with black eyes, dark hair, and a weird name.

That night, Dad was away on his out-of-town job, and Sebastian was fast asleep. When Sebastian heard that Mom had him from his baby days, he seemed to have relaxed and went to sleep almost immediately.

As for me, the floodgates of my mind were kicked open. I could not sleep with all this new information. I could see that my mom's bedroom light was on as well. One mom loved me and left me. The other brought me to a different world and always worried about my leaving her.

One mom was sick, maybe dead. The other I had wished in my anger to leave me alone and go away.

One mom would never be with me. Was it my fault? What if I had not wanted to come to Canada? There were too many thoughts in my mind.

I decided to walk to her room. Mom was sleeping with a book on her face and the lights on.

"Mom," I said.

"Yes dear," replied mom with closed eyes. The open book slipped to the front of her neck.

"Mom, I made my decision. I want to be your Dean, not Enrique."

Her half-opened eyes were glassy.

"Sure, we will celebrate your new name when Father comes. Now, go to sleep, my little Dean."

Under the Baobab Tree

We moved to a new house when I was in grade three. In our new yard stood a huge tree. My father told me this tree was a symbol of prosperity and no matter what happened to the rest of the garden, this tree was never to be cut.

As a child who had spent a mere seven years and eight months on the earth, the tree assumed majestic mystic significance. I truly believed what my father said. I remember watering the huge tree with my sand bucket every day for a couple of weeks or so.

You have to know how our baobab tree looked. It was huge all right, but it had funny looking strong branches coming from the lower third of its trunk. These were the branches that we could swing on. The trunk had two squirrel holes. A busy black squirrel was often seen entering one of these holes. On its north face, green moss grew on its bark. My guide leader had told us that if we got lost in a forest, we should look for moss growing on the tree trunks because that signified the north. So, our baobab tree had a north face with moss growing on it and about the middle wild orchids made it their home, intertwining around the trunk. These orchids had actually been transplanted by my father. They had the very nice name of "Venus's slippers"!

The best part of this tree was not its visual impact but the sensational sounds it generated. Let me see—I can count eleven sounds. Maybe in those days I knew more. The rustling of leaves, when a soft evening breeze blew westwards; a busy woodpecker's tic-toc; raindrops falling from upper branches to lower, and then into a puddle underneath; chameleons hissing over the bark; the wind chime singing a sweet tone, or the wind chime making angry confused songs when air currents were strong. The best sounds came from finches and sparrows gathered in the evening. They would not sing. They would chatter as if there had been a meeting called and they had to finish their social talk prior to a formal gathering.

This tree symbolized that part of life which is very meaningful to me. Every night after dinner, we would sit around the tree to talk or sing. My grandmother would take the important role of arbitrator. She had to decide which of the children excelled in telling the scariest story, who cheated on a card game, or who pulled practical jokes. She took her job seriously. There was only one universal punishment for all the cheaters and losers: they had to massage her legs for an enormous length of time.

Apart from collective activities, I used the baobab tree as my confidante. After my father died, the tree acted as a father substitute. This tree knew all about my dreams, plans and anguish. It admirably stood my practicing for auditions for school dramas, and my singing. My first love letter was opened under this tree and my Spanish lesson was practiced there with zeal.

After twenty-two years of absence, I visited my hometown again. The house itself had changed hands twice. I knew the new owners but they were away on a holiday. I needed to see my baobab tree.

I circled the house. It was well maintained with a manicured garden. At first, I could not see the baobab tree, and my heart sunk. However, it was there. It had something else stuck on it, oh yes; it looked like a tree house. It was a perfectly carpentered tree house, and my tree graciously held it in its arms.

Should I enter the grounds?

I did.

Hello, my tree.

Rustle rustle; I definitely heard rustling, as if I was invited.

The rope ladder leading to the tree house looked strong enough to bear my weight, and I climbed the twenty-two steps that led to a small playhouse with a little window.

Even inside the tree house, everything was neat, with a small rocking chair and curtains on the window. The orchids were gone; I did not spot any bird nests either.

I was in the belly of my beloved tree. It was a warm, peaceful feeling; I curled up inside the womb of my baobab, not at all anxious to get down the ladder.

∛

The Power of Silence

No one suspected that such a healthy looking son of Mrs. Singh could be deaf. Even his mother did not realize it until he was almost three years old. She always believed that he was stubborn (which he was) and manipulative, too; that was her husband's interpretation.

Ranbir Singh (a.k.a. Munna) had the most beautiful and expressive eyes in the Singh household. He also had longer eyelashes than his sister, and a piercing, watchful gaze. One can almost say that Munna's eyes saw, heard, and spoke. Alas, the language that those pair of eyes spoke seemed to be meant only for him.

On his third birthday, he was given a toy lawnmower, which made so much noise that even the children at the birthday party covered their ears. Munna seemed unperturbed. That was the point when his mother started worrying about his hearing and his lack of speech.

The Singh household was loud, with different types of sounds competing. Mrs. Singh and grandmother had their religious tapes on whilst they cooked for the family. Reena, a fifteen-year-old sister of Munna, had her Walkman or favorite radio station on. Munna's only brother, Jaswir, had the television on almost twenty-four hours a day with the sports channel blasting. Mr. Singh, who was a mechanic by profession, always had a car or two in the garage to work on. He had to have the news station on his radio at full throttle whilst he worked. In all this chaos of sounds, no one noticed that Munna was not cueing to any of them.

On the night after the birthday party, Mrs. Singh whispered to her husband, "I am so worried there is something wrong with our son."

As usual, Mr. Singh missed the point his wife was making. "Sure there is something wrong; if you watch the sports channel all day, you're bound to miss everything else in life."

"I am not talking about Jaswir, you know, but about Munna," continued Mrs. Singh.

"What about him? He had such a nice birthday party." Quite a typical response from Mr. Singh.

"Sure, but did you notice his behaviour? All the other cousins were playing, and that awful lawn mower was making so much noise, yet he did not seem to mind at all."

"Oh, that." Now Mr. Singh was interested and offered his opinion. "If you ask me, he behaved very well, in contrast to your sister's brats."

Mrs. Singh sighed. She did not want to continue this conversation, knowing in the end it would have been proven that her sister did not know how to control children, was raising them with the most permissive attitude and was turning them into little beasts fit to be reared in the wilderness.

The next day was typical for the Singh household, with one little difference: it was the last day of school for Jaswir and Reena. Although Reena did not want her to, Mrs. Singh had insisted upon picking her up from the school. As usual, Munna was accompanying mother.

Students started appearing slowly on the school grounds. Most of them had lots to carry, as they had emptied their lockers and some had gifts from departing friends. Reena was nowhere to be seen. Mrs. Singh looked around. She was the only woman who was dressed differently, in her ethnic pantsuit. Other mothers seemed to be casually dressed. Mrs. Singh looked at her bejeweled hands with the six golden bracelets and gold chain, and thought, *No wonder Reena does not want me to come to the school.*

Just then, a soft voice spoke to her. "Hello. May I touch your scarf? It is so lovely." A delicate looking, smiling face was addressing her.

"Oh, it is nothing." *What am I saying?*, thought Mrs. Singh.

The smiling face was still chatting, "And what a lovely boy you have. Look at his eyelashes; girls would die to have eyelashes like that!"

Mrs. Singh knew that she was feeling shy and did not know how to expand on this enjoyable conversation. Munna suddenly broke that awkward moment.

He started grunting and flapping his arms, like a chicken dancing. His mother knew that whenever he got excited, he had to express it by jumping up and down or flapping his arms like a bird. Munna had spotted not his sister, but a lawn mower!

All this excitement for a lawn mower? Why?

Meanwhile, the kind face was now looking at Munna intently. Within the next few minutes, Reena arrived; the kind face thrust a card in her hands and invited her to the community health unit meeting.

After arriving at home, Ms. Singh got involved in their daily routine. She had to gather courage to ask a crucial question of her mother-in-law (bai-ji).

"Bai-ji, do you remember when your children were small?"

"Of course, I do. What a question," retorted Bai-ji.

"I really worry about Munna, and wonder if he will ever speak; and I'm not sure if he hears us," Mrs. Singh meekly added.

"How can you even think that? In our Singh household, everyone hears and talks, if anything a little bit too well. Even in your family, your sister's children are so loud that that surely is not the problem," Bai-ji taunted.

Why does it always have to end with my sister's children? Mrs. Singh sighed inwardly.

"You know, when the other children were already asking questions and singing, Munna was so quiet," said Mrs. Singh, pouring out her worries.

"Now hush, don't you know boys always talk later than girls? And there were more girls at the birthday party," her observant mother-in-law offered.

"Even so, I think something is wrong," muttered Mrs. Singh.

The phone rang. It was her sister asking permission to leave her five-year-old daughter and seven-year-old son with Mrs. Singh whilst she shopped. Her sister was in a hurry, as usual.

"Wait, of course you can bring the children, but I must ask you a question," Mrs. Singh urged over the phone.

But this only sister of Mrs. Singh was born with roller skates on her feet. She did everything in a rapid sequence, talking, walking, cooking, and giving advice.

"You worry for nothing. I would give anything for my children to be silent for one day. Enjoy all this whilst it lasts." She was soon off the hook.

Let me try Reena. She reads big books and watches all the health shows. She felt ashamed that she had to treat Reena as an adult. But what could she do? All the adults she'd tried to talk to had no time for her worries.

"Reena, come over here and watch this," and Mrs. Singh asked her daughter to observe Munna who was as usual playing with his trains. He could amuse himself with "Thomas the Tank Engine" for literally an hour. Previously she had considered this a good thing, since she could then accomplish other tasks.

"Mom, are you being silly? He is just playing with the train," Reena replied.

"Oh, not that—look at the way he is lying down and watching the train."

"Mom, for God's sake, I have a lot to do. Do you want me to take the train from him?"

"No," said the helpless Mrs. Singh.

The next two days were very difficult for her. She tried several sounds when Munna was playing. Sometimes, she tried to shock him by ringing a bell loudly; other times, she purposely sat him next to her in the kitchen when she operated the food mixer. Munna's responses varied. At times, he would look at her with inquisitive eyes, and on one occasion, he covered his ears and seemed distressed. Mrs. Singh was partially happy. *He can hear then!* she thought.

She decided to try the religious route. She started fasting on various days. She was informed by her mother-in-law that a certain deity might help with Munna's speech. To appease that goddess, she had to take a vow of silence. How ironic!

Friday was assigned to be the day of silence. She had to observe eleven Fridays without speaking, remaining in complete silence. The first week proved to be an impossible ordeal. There were visitors, and her long forgotten friends insisted on speaking to her on the phone. Moreover, Munna became very anxious and clingy with her.

By the third week, she found a new way to cope with this situation. She would carry a notebook around her neck and would reply in writing. When the fifth week approached, she became very good at ignoring sounds around her, especially her husband's snoring and mother-in-law's sly remarks.

On the sixth Friday, she decided to clean her wardrobe, as her room was the only quiet sanctuary. She came across an unfamiliar visiting card, a Mrs. Bellings, who was supposedly a communication specialist. *Where did I get that card? Ah yes*, she remembered, *it was given to me by that kind, smiling white lady*. The card read, "For all problems regarding children's communication difficulties please contact our office at

XXXXXX."

With a sudden burst of inner energy, Mrs. Singh decided that she would phone that kind lady. But she could not do so due to her vow of silence. Quickly, she wrote a note for Reena to call the number and make an appointment. Reena reluctantly phoned and left a message to call Mrs. Singh at home.

The week passed amidst hope and anxiety. Mrs. Singh was hopeful that the kind lady would get help for Munna, but was worried that she would not be able to effectively communicate in her broken English.

The Friday morning summer day was quiet. The children were still sleeping and Mr. Singh had already left for work when the telephone rang. Mrs. Singh's first impulse was to break her vow of silence, but as she approached the phone in the corridor, her jaw dropped.

Munna was holding the phone and talking: "Hello, hello, Mum."

Mrs. Singh drowned her vow of silence in happy tears.

CΩ

Technoforest

There was nothing distinctive about the eight-story building of the M. General. The seventy-five-year-old brick exterior stood fast through many severe winters and torrential rains. The architectural design was precise, exactly twenty-five windows, three balconies, and a covered terrace from second to sixth stories. The top was also used for emergency helicopter landings. Therefore, the seventh story did not have fancy covered terraces.

Out of the four entrances to the M. General, the east entrance was identified as the main entrance to Emergency. Recently, the hospital staff as well as the patients had been assigned a smoking area, which was ironically quite close to the main entrance. From Emergency, one could take several paths. A red line, which ended in the ICU, delineated one of the paths; the yellow line headed for the x-ray department, and there were other lines leading to this or that other department. However, one path was called the "baby bear path." Whoever thought this up must have been quite a creative person. There were the little pink and blue paw prints of a baby bear leading to the area known as "Premies and Growers."

One started walking on this little bear path, and that

suddenly led to a kind of open space which swallowed up this little bear path in a high-ceilinged playroom with lots of sunshine. Beyond that open space, the illusion of being in a playforest vanished. It suddenly led to a number of rooms, with lots of healthy professionals moving around, wearing sinister or tired expressions. This inner cave had an all-round viewing area, through which glimpses of another world could be caught.

Sara always thought that she was seeing an episode from a science-fiction movie. She had visited paediatric wards, but this was different. There were no yelling, wailing babies. There was a background of white noise, a distinct hum from suction apparatus, only interrupted by suddenly chirping alarms from little tents.

There was an inner protected sanctuary. All visitors were required to wash their hands well up to their elbows and scrub them, and wear surgical gowns and gloves prior to visiting precious treasures hardly measuring in length to an outstretched adult palm—some weighing less than 1500 grams!

Where is my precious bundle? She glanced around.

Where is my very own little fighter? Sara moved silently amongst these tents, tubes, machines and professionals. She could hear her own breathing, and for the first time felt awkward about her lungs processing airflow so well. What right had she to breathe so well when her flesh and blood was gasping for air and completely dependent on assistance to take those small, precious breaths of life? With new insight into her own breathing, Sara almost choked.

Is this what one describes as survivor's guilt? Why my little David, why not me?

"Ms. Ferguson, could you please come to the office after your visit? We have to talk to you about a decision." David's nurse was talking to her.

"Yes, of course," Sara could hear herself mumbling.

I have to be strong for David; Sara was practicing self-talk. Now she was almost at David's cot. His tent was covered with a quilted blanket Sara had made herself, and around David she had placed family photographs of her, his father, and David's sister Melissa. In another family photograph were David's grandparents with Sara and David, Sr., a picture taken last Christmas when Sara was clearly very pregnant.

Heart filled with great compassion and sorrow, she lifted the cover on the bed and the tent.

"Darling, Mom is here, wake up," Sara heard herself saying.

One lazy eyelid lifted.

"Daddy could not come today, but Mommy brought a tape recorder and Daddy whistled into the microphone..."

The right-hand pinky moved and Sara was thrilled at the response.

"Melissa made two drawings, one of a clown and the other of a rainbow. She will come with Daddy," the one-sided conversation continued.

Sara perceived a frown on David's forehead. I am sure he is annoyed, she thought to herself.

Oh dear, what should I do? Sara fussed with the bedside notes and instructions. There was another message for her to contact the neonatologist on duty.

"David, Mom will return in a few minutes." Sara touched David's right foot and he moved it ever so slightly as if in acknowledgement.

She knew the neonatologist's office so well. They'd had family meetings prior to David's heart surgery and that room meant something sinister to her. David's neonatologist was a man of indeterminate age; depending on his stress level, he looked young or old. Roughly, he must have been in his early forties. He was always attired in sterile hospital gowns and had this green cap on. He talked with much intensity and usually had lots of pamphlets for them. Today, he seemed different—he actually smiled. Sara noticed that he had a very fresh smile, a Colgate smile!

Dr. Mercer said to her, "David has proven himself to be a good fighter. He is breathing on his own, and his blood metabolites are coming to a normal range. If he maintains this, we could move him to Growers."

Sara was in disbelief. David would have been the first infant of this batch of Premies out of the intensive section to move to Growers. The Growers section was reserved for infants who, in spite of their prematurity, made it. Growers allowed them to grow at their own rates, but more importantly, the parents now could handle them, hold them to their hearts, sing to them, and feed them!

Dr. Mercer was explaining to her that some infants sometimes have to be brought back to the intensive unit. He was advising her to talk to the social worker so that arrangement could be made for David to return home. Dr. Mercer continued, "I do not want you to think that David will be discharged soon. Some Premies take a longer time in Growers. We should project one month from now...."

Sara was already fiddling with her cell phone, which had to be off near the special care nursery. She thanked Dr. Mercer and made a beeline for the outdoor playground where she was allowed to use her cellular.

"Hello, David."

At the other end Sara could hear a gasp. For the past ten weeks, telephones had been scary for both of them. For David, Sr., a call from his wife was especially alarming.

"What is the matter, Sara, why don't you talk?" demanded David, Sr.

"Don't worry, we, our son, will be in Growers soon."

"Jolly good, Sara! You know what you're saying, don't you?"

"Of course. When will you visit us? Do not forget to pick up Melanie from the babysitters. You know we should celebrate today as David's real birthday."

"Okay, okay." Poetic kind of talk did not suit David, who was a practical man.

Sara gathered new energy from somewhere. For the first time, she did not think scrubbing her hands up to the elbows was an ordeal. She even hummed whilst doing this too-familiar activity. David was waiting for her. He was alert and moved his little fingers and toes more than he normally did. Sara thought she saw him smiling. She pulled a nurse who was nearby to confirm that "smile." However, the nurse must not have been having a good day, and flatly stated that it was only a grimace, which was supposedly a pain response. Normally, Sara would have been angered by such a blunt answer, but today was the birthday of her son. She decided that it was a smile that she saw and nothing else.

David was unconcerned and decided to go back to sleep.

A wet blouse reminded Sara that the time had come for her breast bump routine, to store nourishment for her precious treasure.

Sara chuckled at the thought that technoforests still had milky rivers.

ᘓ

Mr. Sabarwal, His Green Parrot and I

Our basti* has every thing. We have houses made up of cement blocks, and crumbling wooden houses, too. We have a Hindu temple, a mosque,† and a gurudwara‡ within a stone's throw from each other. We have cars that run on petrol and trucks that only work on diesel, at least seventy bicycles, and a bullock cart.

Our market day is Friday. This is the day when one socializes and gossips. The main street takes a completely different turn on market day. There are vendors everywhere, children play on the streets, and challenging chess games are constantly taking place on the roadside, except of course during the rainy days. If you do not have money to buy sweets, all you have to do is show the café proprietor how hungry you are, and that you are feeling very weak. Everyone knows that he has a soft spot for the children; he simply cannot bear any child crying. So, you can see that Fridays are the best days for any who child who lives in the Kurbani Basti. That is a suburb of the

---

* basti: a small suburb
† mosque: Holy prayer place for Muslims
‡ gurudwara: Holy prayer place for Sikhs

big city of Jalalpur in the Indian state of Uttarpradesh,* in case you have forgotten your geography.

Let me also tell you what we do not have. We children would like a movie theatre, our very own. We do not have a swimming pool. We have a game farm where we can see some animals. However, we do not have a proper zoo. Some people in the basti keep fish in their private pools. I have seen two peacocks in a rich man's yard. But, I have never seen or heard of anyone having an amazing parrot like Mr. Sabarwal has.

I have told you about all the things we have. I forgot to tell you about two schools we have. No, three schools if you count a school run by the nuns. (My mother tells me that they do witchcraft, and it is not really considered a school.) There is a girl's school and a boy's school. The schools have a high wall separating them. Even then, some foolish boys always try to climb the wall. One boy recently broke his leg. Unfortunately, he fell into the girl's compound. These girls did not help him at all. They just laughed at him and giggled. If it had not been for the peon, he would probably have lain there for days, as it was the weekend. I go to that boy's school and I am in grade six. I am really good in sports and I am also a good runner and a good swimmer. The reason I am telling you all this is because there is a connection between Mr. Sabarwal, his parrot and I.

This parrot is not like the ones that fly in the hundreds in the blue skies during harvest season. This parrot is much larger, probably overfed. He has a sharp red beak and a beautiful crest on his head, somewhat like a little cap on his forehead. The amazing thing about this parrot is that he talks almost like we do. He even seems to know secrets in one's mind. He can make

---

* Uttarpradesh: a northern state in the republic of India

you feel guilty within two minutes flat. The first day when Mr. S (we call Mr. Sabarwal by that name and he does not mind) asked me to come to his house, the parrot greeted me, saying, "Hey, do not touch that chair, sit." And after a while, when I was eating a sweet offered by Mr. S, the parrot seemed to scold me for making a mess! It grunted and fussed as if I were doing that on purpose. It is true that I dropped some crumbs on the floor. But I had never been scolded by a parrot before in my entire life. I have had scoldings from my sisters, brother, father and servants, and even from teachers. But never before from a parrot, who is caged and merely twenty inches long. I have never felt so humiliated in my entire life. From that moment on, we became sworn enemies. I like to talk and brag about my enemies. Unfortunately, I do not think my friends would agree with me if I told them that this parrot had become my number one enemy!

On that first encounter, no matter where I sat in Mr. S's living room, this parrot controlled me with his watchful eyes. It actually has a human name. Mr. S calls him "Tippu Sultan". If you ask me, this is a totally inappropriate name for a parrot. Tippu was the greatest warrior in his time.* But this two-feather-crested bird? Besides, Tippu is a better name for a dog. I meekly said to Mr. S that his parrot could have a better name. Mr. S is a scientist. He gave me a long lecture on how his parrot associates sounds and may not respond to him if he changed his name. I thought that the explanation was far-fetched. My sister got married last year. They changed her last name and the first name too. When she came home she knew exactly who she was. Now, I am not comparing my sister with this parrot, but you can see the logic, can you not?

The reason I had gone to Mr. S's house was to sell the worms

---

* Tippu Sultan: a well known warrior in Indian history

for his fish. Previously, my older brother used to do this job. He is working now. He had decided that I should take on some responsibility. Thus, my biweekly visits had started.

Mr. S lived with Tippu. Everything was geared around Tippu. Tippu lived in a cage, which was made of brass. He also had a hanging bar outside, where he liked to swing. He needed fresh water every day. He also was given a bath every day. If Mr. S brought Tippu's dinner late, he used to have a temper tantrum. I am told that on one day, Tippu refused to eat until Mr. S apologized. There were literally hundreds of Tippu's pictures all over Mr. S's House. Tippu listens only to soft music, and if he does not like the music, he will shriek, and flutter and shriek some more and fret.

The real reason for my talking about Tippu and I is the incident on May the 23rd. It was the summer holiday, and I was supposed to be delivering live fish roe for Mr. S's ugly Gouramis. It was the kind of job I did not like. I have also told you about the animosity that existed between Tippu Sultan and me.

I entered the house by the back door. I was totally surprised to find that the door was not locked. The house was like a silent dream where one knows that something is happening but no one knows what the actual event will be.

I tiptoed further, and almost slipped on the wet floor. What a sight! There were big fat gouramis* and gold fish all over the floor. Accidentally, I crushed one angelfish from the tank. The huge fish tank, which was a showpiece of Mr. S's household, was broken into four or five big pieces. It appeared as if someone

* gouramis: a type of fish

had hit the tank with a big bamboo stick. A small plastic mermaid who sat in the bottom of the fish tank blowing air bubbles from her cupped hands was amongst the dead fish. Her plastic smile looked quite pathetic in this morbid scene. There were other items scattered from the fish tank: precisely twelve shells of various shapes, one plastic mermaid, a plastic fisherman toy with a fishing rod still in his hands, lots of sand of different colors, plastic leaves and real moss, and water plants, and a shining diamond ring (imitation of course).

There was further evidence that house had been entered and burglared. I had this cold sensation arising from my throat, creeping underneath my skin and then going though all the cells of my body. What was I supposed to do? Should I run and call the neighbours, or first see what happened to Mr. S? I almost chose to run away but a weak whimper stopped me. It was surely Tippu Sultan who was trying to say something. Where was he? I scanned the room .The room was dark because the lights were off. I reached for the switch but the lights would not work. I opened the curtain to get some rays of light from the outside street lamp—and I saw him there.

The great Tippu Sultan was lying on his side on something big and black .His wings were cut. Both his legs were tied with strong red string. He was bruised all over. It seemed as if he had been involved in a big fight. He seemed like a beaten and fallen war hero. He was not moving.

A street car passed. Suddenly, there were some rays of light, which reluctantly entered though the window curtains that I had opened, and I caught sight of those eyes. My enemy's eyes. My proud enemy's sharp eyes. I could understand the language of those eyes, without ever having any training in the psychology of parrots. Those eyes were humble, they were urging me. They were inviting me. I accepted the invitation. In a split second I knew that my enemy was inviting me to help his master, who was lying motionless on the floor. Mr. S was seriously beaten. He lay unconscious on the floor amongst his prized fish. Tippu was actually sitting on his chest as if to protect him from invaders. The black mound was Mr. S wearing his black pullover.

The rest of the story is history that has given me the title of a hero in our basti. I do not know how many times I have given the account of my brave actions in alerting neighbours and indirectly saving Mr. S's life.

Mr. S is very grateful to me. I was allowed to enter his house and feed his new fish, in their even larger fish tank.

As far as my relationship with Tippu, who also survived the traumatic incident, well, it is not that good. I could conquer Tippu Sultan only for fifteen seconds, when he needed me to protect his master. I think he resents me even more than before, as Mr. S gives me more attention now. His eyes and shrieks suggest that he considers me an unwanted visitor. Oh, well. You cannot always please a lame, jealous green parrot.

ᙣ

Life Lies in Forgotten Memories

Throughout my childhood, my parents always shared their memories and recollections of their rich and vivid past. After telling even small anecdotes, my parents' faces seemed revitalised and elated. Even at my young age, my parents, especially my mother, taught me that the richness of life lies in memories. To this day, I am constantly being enlightened by their wonderful stories. Just a few days ago, my mother told me something I had never known before about my family's history. It was one night after dinner when this Arabian Night-like fairy tale was told, never to be forgotten.

Before India came under the rule of the British, it consisted of many princely states. Each state was very different from the others, and boasted and displayed its richness and power in various ways. States were not ruled by dukes and earls, but were under the control of "maharajas," or princes. Many of these maharajas lost their kingdoms soon after British occupation, and others at the time of Independence in 1947. But the maharajas continued to live in glory and splendour for many years. Some of the glory can only be pictured in our minds as it was so fabulous. The maharajas and their families continued to live in beautifully designed palaces whose elegance and richness can now only be seen in paintings and history books. These royal residences stretched over thousands of green acreages. The commoners were not permitted to enter those royal residences. However, there were some exceptions.

To my surprise, my mother's family was very well acquainted with the Maharaja of Mallipur (a small state situated in the west of India). In fact, my mother spent most of her summer holidays living with this royal family. This maharaja had a glorious estate nestled between a calming river and an enchanted forest. The yard was dotted with elegant peacocks, and white doves were commonplace sights in the royal gardens. There were several guest houses and my mother spent many of her holidays in one of them. The main house was restricted to the royal family members. However, guests were allowed to enter the palace for dinners and other social functions. There were two entrances to the maharaja's residence.

The main entrance was adorned with tiger and bear skins on the walls. Even the white, marbled floors were covered with rich carpets and animals skins. All kinds of polished hunting gear were lined up symmetrically on these walls. They looked bright and unused, but anyone who had even the slightest knowledge of the Maharaja of Mallipur understood that this was not the case. He was an avid hunter and he often got my great-grandfather to follow him on his trips.

The sturdy, wooden door which opened to this collection welcomed only men. Another entrance was to be used by women and children under the age of ten. The women's entrance was east of the main hall and was just as extravagant as the main entrance, except that it had a much more serene and relaxing atmosphere. This entrance was always guarded by a woman whose job was to verify that all women had their heads well covered by some type of silk cloth before they entered the palace. The palace's richness did not lie entirely in the two entrances, nor in the main hall—it was also in the fountain located near the dining areas.

My mother always used to call it the "magical" fountain. The calming sound of the cascading water and the sweet breezes from the balcony behind it created a safe and placid milieu. Beyond the fountain, a large window overlooked the cashew nut orchards.

My mother shared fond memories of playing on the banks of the river where the cashew nut tree stood. She would secretly climb the trees in order to get the best pick of cashews. Unfortunately, even though she wanted to keep this to herself she could not, since the sap of the cashew fruits had burned her face! Her face was swollen for many weeks, and she felt very guilty and learned her lesson the hard way! This was just one of the many anecdotes my mother had to disclose.

A few events that my mom told me about are definitely worth mentioning. She described to me the winter pigeon races that took place after the rainy season. All the members of the royal family collected on the open balcony where these white pigeons were kept in ornate, wooden mini-palaces. They were fed and trained very well. The pigeon keeper had a very important social standing. If his pigeon won a race then the pigeon keeper would be rewarded with gold and silver. The winning pigeon had a silver ball around its neck. I think this must have been a fascinating race. Whilst pigeons raced, the owners sat anxiously on the balcony. There was always a lot of excitement over the finish. However, the excitement did not end there.

The kite ceremony was also a remarkable springtime event.

Boys of all ages would eagerly climb the hills surrounding the palace to fly their handmade kites. During this time, there were many shops which sold kites for those who could not manage to make their own. My mother was not very happy with these games because girls could not fly the kites during this festive time. Instead, they were told to help the boys make the kites. The girls were not at all pleased by this injustice but they still managed to have their own fun.

The girls of the palace had one game from which the boys were restricted. The boys tried their very best to be included but they were prohibited. This was the famous "doll marriage." The girls used to arrange their dolls' marriages with great ceremony. The dolls were adorned with flower garlands. Sweets were distributed to all the invited guests. Even disputes at the time of the marriage were acted out. Sometimes, the adults had to intervene when the bride's and bridegroom's relatives began to quarrel. My mother said that she did not agree with games like that from her childhood as they created inequality between men and women. The bride's company was always made to be inferior to the bridegroom's and my mother never liked this inequality right from an early age. However, this was the custom and women were considered inferior to men for many generations in India and, at the time, around the changing world. Change it did.

My mother did return to the state of Mallipur a few years ago and brought along my two brothers, as I was not yet born. The palace was there but had been converted into a hotel, as had been the fate of many smaller palaces in India. The hundreds of acres of greenery were now a cement jungle and the calming river no longer warbled happily. Instead, its tunes were of sorrow and pain. Two peacocks roamed around as an attraction to the guests rather than as dignified household members. The "magical" fountain was replaced by a row of courtesy phones for the guests. The palace no longer had its magical abilities; the surroundings were dismal and worrisome. I could feel the sadness in my mother's voice as she reminisced over this childhood memory and the events thereafter.

Following that evening, I felt that same enlightenment as I always did after my parents would share a memory. However, this time it not only enlightened me, it affected me as I began to realize how things can change. Past glories can quickly decay into oblivion. The richness of life, however, lies in memories, which often lie forgotten but can surface to bring back magical moments.

છ

A Tale of Royal Blues & A Moonlight Sonata

She felt quite overdressed. The long black velvet gown, nightshade nylons and stilettos were just not her. She did not mind the string of pearls. Her curly auburn hair was getting stuck in the shell brooch of her evening dress. Every now and then, she had to give a little shake to get the hair strands out.

The plaza was now humming with activity. Couples well-dressed in the best manner looked like little pawns on a huge chess set. They moved mechanically, smiled only occasionally and whispered instead of speaking.

What was she doing with these folks? This picture was not right. She was a definite misfit. An alien on the planet called Hypocrisy. Curiously enough, the planet seemed to be right whenever Charles was with her. Without him, she imagined herself like a kite without a string. No direction, no aim, no claim in this hypocritical, hostile planet of the rich and famous.

Jane was becoming increasingly aware of curious, lazy stares draped on her bare shoulders. "Where are you?" Jane was asking silently of the still absent Charles. "The concert starts in fifteen minutes and after the third bell, no one will be allowed to enter the concert hall."

Take courage. Don't be hasty. Charles will be here. Jane tried some self-talk. After all, he had spent a lot of money on these tickets and it was entirely his idea.

"A rose for you, miss." An eager flower vendor offered a beautiful red rose from his fragrant basket.

"No, no, I do not want it." Jane replied.

She was quite shocked by the huskiness in her voice. Was she going to lose her voice when her mind was nearly blown away? Two more ladies asked directions for the box office and a young man asked her if she had a ticket to sell. The third bell rang with such shrillness that Jane was woken up from her daydreaming. Paradoxically, as she tried to root herself in the reality around her, all the humming birds seemed to have gone to sleep. There was a silence only interrupted by the ushers' whispers.

Should she enter the concert hall sans Charles or retire to her familial planet in apartment number 5 on 797, Woodward Street? How could Charles humiliate her so? Oh, selfish, selfish Jane. Maybe he has been in an accident?

Five minutes before the final call, and no Charles. Her blue-green eyes suddenly were transformed into royal blue oceans. The deep oceans covered the sorrow quite effectively. They were experts of a sort in siphoning sorrow. Their effort was only evident in a change of color. Misty green-blue to royal blues! Royal blues unfathomable, and viscous with a concoction of humiliation, sadness and hopelessness.

Over the mist of ocean blue, she could see a white flag. A truce of some sorts? To win back her vanished dignity or to offer a straw to the drowning man?

It was actually a strong brown hand making a delicate gesture, offering her a white handkerchief. Jane took the handkerchief. Her throat was so choked with emotions that she had been rendered speechless.

It was only after a while that she noticed the rest of the person affiliated with that strong, generous hand. The hand was now escorting her inside the concert hall. She was mesmerized. Her light steps reflected the will power of a hand puppet. She followed that hand.

Jane has no recollection of how their seating arrangements worked out, nor can she remember which sonatas were played — until the last.

By the interval, the turbulence in the oceans was pacified. For the first time, Jane had a good look at her silent partner. It was hard to say where this admiration for a strong, generous hand would lead.

She desperately wanted to thank him. This simple idea threw her into a confused state. What was she to say? If she stated, "Thank you," that would really seem very impersonal and business-like. If she uttered, "I am very grateful for your help," she would give the impression that she had been a helpless little wimp. If she said nothing....!

Yes, that is it. Until I find good words, and I do not look like a complete loser, even if that is what I feel I am, I should stay silent, and appear mystified.

This was in a way a good band-aid solution to her broken

ego. Jane was very surprised at herself. She was taking a perverse interest in this intensely bleak situation.

A pregnant pause followed. It could not have been more than ten minutes. To Jane, it lasted 50 million light years.

Beethoven's Moonlight Sonata broke the impasse. She picked out a new language with the floating music notes, embedded in her emotions and his. The solution was simple enough. She only needed to transfer the langue de coeur from her pale white, to his generous brown, hand.

☙

Michael Jackson

Sheila was ecstatic. She was allowed to go out with her three cousins who were visiting from abroad. She always waited for these cousins. Even if one did not count the oldest cousin, who was almost eighteen years old, she could still spend time with Vani, who was thirteen, and Sheetal, who had turned sixteen during the summer.

Everything was admirable about her cousins—the way they dressed, talked, and walked. Best of all, she admired how they dealt with the elders in the family. Vani in particular feared no one. Today she'd told everybody that she simply could not live without watching television! Sheila couldn't imagine saying those things in front of grandpa! She was surprised and secretly admired her cousin for her boldness. That kind of statement from Vani was fairly typical. She insisted that she would like to watch the "Michael Jackson" show advertised for next week and even hinted at going on a hunger strike if she was not allowed to do so. This meant the children had to go to their neighbours, who had a television set. The unspoken fear in everybody's mind was that those nosy neighbours would gossip that there was no discipline in Sheila's household and the girls were lacking moral training!

There was much commotion after her declaration. Papa was not pleased at all. Sheila could read that in the persistent frown on his forehead. At the same time everyone knew he would do anything for his sister's children. Vani's mother passed away in a car accident two years ago. The family never grieved this loss properly. Sheila's father was a twin to Vani's mother, and felt it was his moral responsibility to make his sister's children happy, even if he did not like the free spirit of his nieces.

Sheila's mom could not understand the reason for argument. She had no knowledge of western singers. If Mr. Jackson could recite classical Indian melodies, that would have been another story. Surprisingly, the real opposition came from Vani's sister, who declared that Michael Jackson was the ugliest singer alive and there was no way she was going to watch him.

Sensing this strong oppositional climate, Vani changed her strategies. She would make their visit coincide with one to another uncle in the next township precisely at the time when the Jackson show would be televised. Vani's strategy appeased them all. Sheila's father did not have to say "no" to his favourite niece, Vani did not have to go on hunger strike, and such a "silly" and frivolous activity did not have to be condoned by Grandpa.

This uncle had the latest model of TV and was of a very open disposition. The children were certain that their request would be met without further complications.

All this was planned without Sheila's involvement. She was allowed to go with them purely for economic reasons. Sheila's father's economizing sense dictated that his Jeep would leave home only when it was fully loaded. That meant one empty seat, as Sheila's older sister adamantly refused to go on this trip.

Therefore, Sheila was allowed to travel. It was a terrific day for her. She dressed herself in the best clothes. She wore a long skirt, which was made by a seamstress who believed that clothes should be made to fit for at least three years more than the chronological age of the child. Sheila was almost lost in that pleated skirt. As it was not used other than for festivities, a moldy smell emanated from Sheila and of course the odour of the naphthalene balls that were kept in the cupboard to keep the insects away! Her cousin did not approve of her clothes at all.

"Sheila, you have to become a little bit modern," Vani said. "Wait, I will carry my extra pair of jeans and this really cool shirt. Your sandals are o.k. Your hair! Um! Do not part it in the middle like an old woman."

Vani combed Sheila's hair her own way. To Sheila, it felt as if she was messing up her hair rather than combing it, but she did not protest. She refused to wear the jeans, as she knew that her parents would not approve of them.

The two-hour journey on a very rough road brought them to their uncle's home on the outskirts of Delhi, the capital. The journey itself was filled with a lot of laughter, singing and joking. By the end of the trip, Sheila was envious of her cousins and wished she were living in their world. It seemed to be full of enterprise, challenges, fun and novelty. In contrast, her world was predictable, monotonous and strictly ruled.

Once inside their uncle's home, Sheila was surprised to find other youngsters whom her uncle had invited. They all seemed to know about Michael Jackson. They could talk about his latest records. Sheila reached her height of discomfort when in the middle of conversation, one of the teenagers started walking in a slow, stilted manner. Everyone laughed and praised his gait.

They all called him a moonwalker. Little did she know that this boy and others were copying Michael Jackson and his stylish way of singing and dancing. When her uncle joined as well, she felt completely out of place.

"Stop sulking. Come on and join us. The show will not be aired for half an hour." Vani tried to draw Sheila into their midst. She tried to give her all the information about different songs that this singer had sung and how much he was being paid for his songs; she even gave a practical demonstration of how he danced.

At last, the long awaited program started. Sheila could not stop laughing. There he was, a slim, agile man making grotesque sexual moves. She had never seen anything like that in her entire life, certainly not at the all-girls high school she attended. She was totally amazed at his capacity to undulate, jump and express his feelings through gestures so boldly. How could he move just a part of his body, totally in control of the muscular movements, sing, drag his feet, and yet seemed to be dancing? What did it take for a person to be so totally devoid of fear, shame and guilt and so appreciative of his body?

If Sheila were alone with Vani, she could have asked her all these questions. But her cousin was in her own dream world now.

Vani was totally fixated on the singer's image. One teenager, whom Sheila knew as a very shy and modest boy, was acting as if he was a mini replica of Mr. Jackson. She'd never known that this 15-year-old could dance with so much sensuality. And what was she doing? She felt an urge to move about too. But she was too ashamed to let herself go. Her long pleated skirt would have hindered her movements anyway.

Michael Jackson took her to another world. A world she could never have known. A world where men danced, expressed themselves, and were so candid about their sexual motives. For an adolescent, who never saw other men except her cousins and brothers, this opened doors to a shocking, dangerously appealing world. Her cousins noticed how she seemed totally captivated by the show. They teased her mercilessly.

"Gee, you seem to have fallen for him. I hope you can hear and talk to us," Vani stated in her usual untactful way.

"You have to learn English well to become friendly with him," added her uncle, who always teased Sheila about her accent and poor grammar. This uncle had been an Oxford scholar and encouraged children in the family to learn more about rest of the world and learn English.

Sheila would remember the feeling of liberation and happiness when she watched Michael Jackson for the first time. Later on, she was to watch him dance plenty of times. Every single time she watched him perform, that feeling of liberation came to her. It was neither happiness nor ecstasy. It was not even contentment. The nearest description would be a kitten being allowed to unroll balls and balls of soft lambs' wool to its heart's content. The dance had touched Sheila's inner core, giving her a dimension of experience she never before knew existed.

Summer ended abruptly. A week before her cousins departed, the family arranged a traditional summer picnic on the local riverbank. There was lot of food and much singing was allowed. Everyone but Vani seemed to be enjoying themselves. She wore a serious expression for the most part. Vani took Sheila aside and asked to meet her at the other end of the riverbank.

At first Sheila thought Vani was trying one of her bits of mischief. But Vani was so insistent that in the end Sheila made some excuse and moved away from the crowd.

"What has come over you?" said Sheila.
"Sheila, I am very worried about you," interjected Vani.
"What do you mean, worried about me?" Sheila asked.
"Sheila, you are so innocent, I think you may get into trouble," Vani answered. "They are talking about marrying you to a boy from England and you know, things are different there," Vani continued with a serious look on her face. "Look, Sheila, keep this diary carefully with you. I have written down my address and telephone numbers."

The conversation ended. They were required to be with the family and not allowed to wander off from them. Sheila was feeling kind of curious and tingly in her heart, thinking that she was indeed thought as marriageable material. Why was Vani so upset? Maybe, just maybe, she may be a tiny bit jealous of her little cousin?

Sheila's cousins left for home at the end of summer. Sheila was still at home as her grade 11 teacher had been taken ill and her school had yet to find a replacement. She was willing to attend another school but her parents would not allow her to go to a co-educational facility. Her parents would not allow her to be taught by a male teacher either. Thus, Sheila stayed at home. To pass the time, she woke up late; sometimes she helped her mother in the kitchen, or at other times, listened to the radio, drew, or simply chatted with her friends.

One Saturday, her life changed. She was scolded by her mother for arriving late from her friend's place.

"Where have you been? Do you have any dress sense at all?" Sheila's mom sounded angry when she talked in an excited tone.

Sheila looked at herself. She was wearing her favorite white cotton suit and no one had ever told her that it was a bad choice.

"Go and change into something nice!" Sheila's mom was almost squealing now.

Suddenly, memories of how Vani had scolded her for not being modern came into her mind. Within minutes of her changing her attire, she was asked to serve tea to some unknown guests.

"Oh, oh, so this is your daughter. How lovely she looks!" said this strange woman who was studying Sheila as intently as if Sheila was a frog about to be dissected in a biology lab.

"Our Sheila can speak English and she sings very well," Sheila's mother was boasting, which was embarrassing to Sheila.

That was a sure danger signal. Sheila looked around. She saw the family priest, and a few other elders laughing and joking. From what she could gather, Amit Singh's family had requested Sheila's hand for their son who lived in the United Kingdom. He apparently knew Sheila's cousin, who had highly recommended her. The bridegroom was supposed to be a handsome man earning good wages who even had a house of his own!

Sheila was shown the picture of the prospective bridegroom. The instant she saw the picture, she fell in love with him. His big eyes were inviting her to take on a very challenging life journey together. Even though she had not finished her high school diploma, she consented to get married. The wedding was a hurried matter, so much so that the month of October 1992 left her with very blurred memories. He came, he married her, and he carried her away.

At the age of eighteen, Sheila was married to her Prince Charming, her very first love. She started this journey into the unknown full of desires and hope. As her mother always maintained, Sheila was brought up in a proper way, so she would make a wonderful and dutiful wife who would sacrifice herself for her husband and her family! Sheila started this unknown journey with a weight of expectations that she would be a good daughter and wife.

At nineteen, Sheila attended a local hospital in Essex* three times. The first time, her husband brought her. Her lips were swollen; there was a prominent blue black discoloration on her cheeks, and squeeze marks on her left arm. Sheila's husband convinced the authorities that she had slipped on the kitchen floor while washing the windows. He also gave the impression that Sheila was illiterate and could not understand or speak in English.

They all believed him! Sheila was aghast that such horrible lies could be sold that easily to so-called sophisticated, educated professionals. Anger kept her quiet superficially but with a seething fire within her. *Did they not see her diary? Where is my diary?* The very diary given by her close cousin Vani.

With her chipmunk eyes, she must have looked a sight. Besides, everyone was so busy that no one seemed to have time for her, definitely not for an "illiterate" Asian female who

---

* Essex: a county in the United Kingdom

obviously did not belong to their world. Pride and humiliation kept her from phoning her cousins. Besides, she could not find her diary with all the phone numbers. And most importantly, in her desperate groping she was still able to find hopeful pockets in her husband's promises when he was not drinking.

The second time burned vividly in her memory. Her next door neighbour had to phone the police. The ambulance brought her to Emergency. A young doctor who suspected the truth interviewed her. This time Sheila wove a most unconvincing story about how she had slipped on the kitchen floor. The story was essentially the same as what her husband had presented last time, only with a minor variation. The police were not convinced at all. However, they could not do anything because of Sheila's reluctance to press charges.

The third time was horrible. Her face was completely discolored. Her eyelids were so swollen that she thought she had turned blind. This time the humiliation was so great, she would have preferred to be dead. The neighbours had to snatch her away from her furious husband and bring her to the hospital against his raving protests. Sheila knew it was all over. Her hopes, dreams, aspirations for a happy married life, all shattered in a million small pieces!

She became an automaton. She was examined, questioned, and requestioned, made to sign innumerable forms. She did everything and anything as demanded of her. Nothing mattered. The social worker did call her cousins who were truly upset that Sheila had not confided in them earlier. But even that did not matter. She was a living zombie, whose inner psyche was dead and rotten. She was numb. When the social worker decided to transfer her to the women's shelter, she did not protest. Her cousins were upset that she chose not to return to them, but little did they understand that a dead mind cannot absorb any feelings, even the good ones.

There in the small cubicle which was supposed to be her safe haven, Sheila felt that her world had matched this cubicle by contracting into a small, insignificant molecule. In one year of her marital life, she had been humiliated and treated like an animal. She could not understand—why was so much vehemence directed against her?

"You were lucky to leave India and come here. If it were not for my mother, I would never have married you."

Another time, his cutting words: *"Look at your face. I am not taking you out with me. You spoiled my life now, it is my turn."*

And in the last fight, it was not enough for him to humiliate Sheila alone.

"You and your dull-witted parents, you are all the same. You just try to phone them. They still believe me more than you." He was talking in that rush that accompanies alcoholics when they suddenly have a lucid moment or two.

He was saying the truth, however painful it was. Her parents would never have taken her side. They would have expected her to be a good wife. The truth was that he had not liked her from the beginning. He constantly compared her to other women. He often talked about her dependency on him as repulsive. What was she supposed to do about it? She was not allowed to phone her relatives and she did not have money. Sheila gradually sank into a victim role, waiting for a miracle to happen.

After some time the numbness of her mind lifted. She was

now overshadowed by sadness. *Can a human feel so sad? Can sadness hurt so much? Why does sadness make one so weak?*

Where is my old life? My friends? My dreams? Why can't I feel anything besides this sad feeling? Sheila was becoming totally engulfed in her sadness. She would often double over with a dull ache that originated in her heart and spread all over her body like volcanic ash.

Sheila became obsessed with her feelings. She wanted to feel more than emotional anaesthesia and sadness. She was worried that no other emotions existed in her mind and that she was shrivelled up like a bath sponge wrung dry.

"Sheila, don't sit alone in your room. Come, join us in the TV room," one of the supervisors of the women's shelter was advising.

Like an automaton or a yogi in an out-of-body experience, Sheila walked towards the room where other women were sitting. She wanted to get out of her sad shell but it would not leave her entirely. She had a horrendous desire to pierce it and deflate it. *Can I ever be rid of this sad shell?* With tears in her eyes, she asked herself the same question again and again.

The TV was on. Sheila was not focusing. Suddenly, a familiar voice and feeling grasped her attention. Michael Jackson was dancing. Sheila could step out of her sad shell! She was suddenly liberated, even if that liberation would last for a mere few seconds. The old feelings flooded her mind.

She knew that she had found the key to her lost world. At last she felt hopeful that another experience was waiting for her. She almost took a jump celebrating the arrival of different feelings, and so did Michael Jackson.

Mina's Deductive Power

It was very suffocating in the bus. The passengers were packed like sardines in a tin. What was worse, the lady sitting next to Mina wore a cheap perfume, enough to give a headache to an entire army! As if that torture was not enough, the fishermen sitting on the other side of the bus smelled of rotten squids and rum.

Mina was certain that the young man sitting next to her was a fisherman. Of course, she did not have proof. However, Mina always took pride in judging persons. Her job as an assistant postmistress gave her ample opportunities to meet people. Her boss, the postmaster, lived up to his reputation of being the laziest man alive. He was very punctual in coming to work. But that was all. Once he made his entry, all the jobs were assigned to Mina and the mailman Babu. The postmaster then spent his entire day playing a game called Shatranj—a game similar to chess.

The scenario at work never changed. Mina and Babu working together, sorting the mail, selling postcards, stamps, money orders, etc. The postmaster and his three playmates lost in the ivory kingdom of the queens, the kings, the bishops, the horses and the knaves. The postmaster had inherited the ivory chess board from his grandfather and nearly all the inhabitants of the town knew about it.

Coming back to Mina, she did not seem to mind having to shoulder the responsibility all by herself. She liked the power that flowed with the unofficial role of being a postmistress. And she took pride in her ability to read a person's mind with very little available information. Mina named this her power of deduction. Sherlock Holmes could have been put to test by Mina's deductive powers. She also had another unique skill—she could deliver babies. This skill assured her social standing and gave her the opportunity to know nearly all the women of childbearing age in her town. She may have appeared helpless in this crowded bus, but at the time of bringing a brand new life into this world, none could equal her—except perhaps, the new local doctor and his wife, who was also a trained midwife.

She focused on the gentleman next to her. She certainly had not delivered him. But he looked familiar. She looked for cues to learn more about him. He was a muscular, strong young man in his late twenties, and he was carrying a newspaper that was considered reading material for the elite. She would have expected him to read "Hurricane," a sensational local newspaper, giving thrilling news such as how a cow had given birth to a calf with six legs. She would not have been surprised if he had been reading the third page, the employment opportunity page of that paper. Instead, he was solving a crossword puzzle.

There were only two bus stops before she had a chance to surmise the situation. The opportunity presented. There was a third person who was also as intent in solving the crossword as Mina's mysterious, challenging next-seat neighbour. This third man was standing behind them and studying how the mystery man was performing.

"I think you'd better try 'ponder' instead of..."The stranger was addressing the mysterious young man.

"Redgate," announced the conductor.

"Sorry, I have to go," announced the third man. "Do not forget to bring those books that you promised."

So, this gentleman was a student. Why do students not have well-scrubbed clean faces any more?

At the next stop, there was a sudden influx of children, all belonging to a young pregnant mother. Mina's mysterious man stood up and gave his seat to her. Mina lost sight of him.

It was only after two weeks that she thought of him again. His picture was on the first page of the national newspaper holding a banner, which stated that the students would go on a hunger strike if the government would not make a decision regarding fee hikes. It was definitely the same man who had been sitting next to her in the crowded bus solving the crossword puzzle. He seemed fierce with his muscular arms and open angry mouth. Mina did not know why she had developed such antipathy to him. He represented something that she was reacting to. He invoked a sense of familiarity in her. That bothered her. Mina's deductive power was of no use to her.

Where are these feelings coming from? Her rational mind was in control again. I do not know this man. He is half my age. I do not even care about him. I did not know him two weeks ago. What is up with me? The questions started pouring from the filter of her rational mind to her irrationally angry outer mind. She decided to get busy and forget about the episode.

Next day was unusually busy for their post office. There were cards and letters and parcels to sort out. Many of the letters did not have addresses on them; yet Mina's deductive power could solve those problems in a jiffy.

Take for example a letter addressed to "Langara (lame boy), behind mosque, can be found in the evenings, if not try the smoke shop!" The second one was more interesting, addressed to: "Phoolmati Rai, the second lane, Alibaug." This address was not too bad, except that the addendum stated, "Post master, make sure that the witch does not get this letter." Mina chuckled. She knew about the story of Phoolmati's mother-in- law who was considered to be a witch. This letter was definitely from Phoolmati's brother. Everyone knew that Phoolmati's mother-in-law was illiterate. Mina's deductive power was working.

"Masterji*, come and help today. There is so much work today," Mina urged the postmaster.

"Minabeti, I will join you as soon as I resolve this problem," referring to a checkmate situation.

Mina felt betrayed. Why is it that all these men are enjoying themselves when she is carrying the full workload all by herself? She thought that she was better off delivering babies. However, with the strong family planning movement and the new town hospital, she was not in as much demand as before. Besides, she thought, this rush at the post office must be temporary. After all, she'd had time to knit two sweaters last month.

---

* Masterji: respectful way of addressing one's boss

The second batch of letters was different. It was actually unusual for this post office to be receiving official looking letters, as illiterate fishermen and their equally illiterate families mostly inhabited the town.

One of the letters came from England. It was addressed to a Mr. J. Kalia, Esq. She could not recall anybody of that name having come to collect letters. Still, the name sounded somewhat familiar.

Within the next few minutes the suspense was cleared. The same young man with angry mouth, muscular arms and a zest to solve crossword puzzles appeared. Mina saw him but acted as if he was insignificant.

"Hmmm. I beg your pardon, ma'am. I have some important mail arriving." The mystery man was speaking in a steady but polite voice.

"Can you not see that I am busy?" Mina snapped without making eye contact.

"I wondered, if I could collect my mail, as I was passing by…" the youth was interrupted.

"What is your name mister?" inquired irritable Mina.

"Oh, sorry, I should have introduced myself. I am Mr. Kalia. I teach at the community college," replied the mystery man.

Mina must have given him one of her most piercing, disapproving looks. Now, it was his turn to apologize again.

"You know, most people do not know or remember me. But

you would probably remember my father who used to work on the government fishing boat many years ago…"

Mina's head was now bursting with memories. It was as if this young man unlocked a memory path that was not accessible before.

"He died during a fishing accident in high seas," The young man continued.

Mina could not hear anymore. Slowly, the memories of the fishing accident came to her. She could visualize the dead fisherman's muscular arms, the rum bottles lying on the beach where the drinking party took place prior to the accident. She also remembered the warmth of those muscular arms and the arrogant promises that she had been given.

"My mom raised me in the town where her folks live, and she changed my name too. After she died, I decided to return…" He was explaining.

Mina could only hear parts of the conversation. Her lonely heart ached terribly.

The only solace was that her deductive power was there, safe and sound.

CB

Blue Grotto

It was a breathtaking scene. From nowhere, an ethereal picture befitting Botellini's paintings appeared. The captured ocean within the underground cave was absolutely still and mirrored every stalactite, so that an unsuspecting viewer might confuse the azure mirror for the real thing. The descriptions in the travel book of a blue grotto did no justice at all. Of course, the books used human lingo.

And this is no human or earthly business at all, thought Bert. *I am glad I joined this tour.*

For a professional photographer like himself, the first instinct was to touch his Nikon to see if it was properly loaded. But there was a prohibition against taking pictures. Usually, he would be so busy fussing with his camera that he would not have noticed every aspect of the scene.

Today was different. He was enjoying this nature's feast with all his senses.

A few minutes passed. He looked around and caught a pair of beautiful brown eyes exploring him. There was mischief and curiosity in those eyes. He felt ticklish. Why were these eyes caressing him all over? He glanced at his socks. This was because in his office his habit of wearing mismatched socks was always joked about. No, that was not it. He was wearing matching navy blue socks.

The pair of eyes now moved closer to him. They belonged to a most exotic looking, stunning woman.

"Are you Mr. Bellini?" she said
"Uh, Yes, but, I do not…"
"No, you do not know me. I have been following you since London."
"What do you mean, following me?"
"Oh, do not worry." She took a small identity card from her purse. "I am Detective Eva. Perhaps we should take a break. There is a nice coffee shop nearby and I can explain everything to you."
"I am sorry, um…Ms. Eva, but I like to keep with my travel schedule."
"I have taken care of everything. In fact, I already told the tour leader that we will join him in Sorrento."

Bert collected himself. *Geese! It was as if this attractive woman was kidnapping him.* However, he realized that he had no willpower to say "No" to this forced relationship.

"I guess it should be o.k. Even so, I need to talk to him."
"Sure, I will wait for you near our bus." She disappeared as quickly as she had appeared.

The guide did not have any objections at all. Whatever she may have told him, it seemed that the guide considered Burt a very lucky man. He even winked and made remarks on how he would never have thought that this serious, almost middle-aged photographer was a romantic in disguise. What followed next was unbelievable.

*   *   *

Sunrays illuminated everything on Burt's antique desk, including specks of dust riding on the rays, and a shiny medallion! Last night's celebrations weighed too heavily upon him. His eyes were still bloodshot from all that drinking. He had a throbbing headache. Even so, it had been a memorable night. His colleagues at the National Geographic, his mother, local friends, and even a new admirer from Brazil had all been there. They'd talked about his adventurous mind and his creative ways to solve a seemingly impossible situation. The mayor had talked about how his medal reflected "environmental heroism." Burt chuckled. Environmental hero indeed!

*   *   *

Burt's mind took him to the blue grotto—his historic meeting with Eva, travelling in her safari Jeep and finding himself on a captivating estate. Eva had convinced him to accompany her on a mission, which basically would exploit his photography skills. In return for his services, he was to receive a handsome sum and an all-paid sailing tour. Secretly, Burt worried about facing a flock of beautiful capricious Italian models.

Soon after arriving at what seemed like a medieval castle, Burt realized that he was not there to enjoy the captivating scene but was a captive himself. He was shown to a chamber where literally hundreds of glass cases harboured reptiles of all kinds.

He was not alone. There was a pale young woman with a troubled look, attired in a white lab coat. She spoke in Portuguese and some broken English, and seemed to be an unwilling participant as well. Eva, who had seemed so charming, changed in this setting. Her eyes never smiled and her pretty looks acquired an eerie quality. Burt was frankly afraid of her.

"Here are the instructions. You have exactly three days to photograph all these creatures. All the photo equipment is in the next room. You will find that it is the latest technology." Eva was speaking like a robot.

"Whatever you need, you have to phone and ask. You are not permitted to leave this room without my consent." A pregnant pause followed. "Any questions?"

"What am I...um...are we supposed to be doing?" Burt felt totally overpowered by this woman.

"This is a project planned by our society for the next millennium. I cannot tell you more. You are here because you are the best wildlife photographer that we could find." Eva turned and vanished, leaving behind the scent of her perfume which by now was giving Bert a severe migraine.

Burt had never seen so many emaciated, shrivelled up and distorted reptiles. What was done to them? One Boa was almost dying. It was one thing to photograph a dying snake in his habitat and completely another scenario to see thousands of reptiles dying in these glass cages. Burt remembered how he had cared for his pet Boa Joker. He had attended innumerable meetings at the city hall to convince his neighbours that Joker was not a public threat. The pain of entrusting his Boa to the SPCA never seemed to cease. Poor Joker had been labeled as a threat to the public safety. Now, he was facing an even grimmer situation. Was he to film and photograph all these dying reptiles?

At that moment, he noticed his assistant Maria. She was crying silently. She said more with her tears than words might have accomplished. She shook her head as if suggesting it was no use to fight these people. In her broken English she told him that she was a biology professor in a prominent Brazilian university and a researcher well known for her contribution toward studies of the genetics of reptiles. Maria had suspected that techniques she had developed were being exploited to alter the genetic makeup of these reptiles. She was worried that Eva's team may have found a way to change non-poisonous varieties into poisonous ones. Maria feared that all the poisonous venom was being used for some ulterior motive that she did not know about.

Until that point Burt had not realized that he was caught in a conspiracy of some sort. Now his intelligent mind visualized many scenarios. One was that a little boy in the pet shop could be endangering himself by buying a supposedly non-poisonous snake that had been altered genetically into a poisonous one. The second scenario would be very potent snake venom used for devious and dubious reasons—chemical warfare perhaps?

Geese! Wake up Bert. He pinched himself. Eva had said everything should be done within three days. This three-day time period was crucial for something. The doors were locked from outside. The adjoining kitchenette faced the steepest fall of that mountainous range. He had to escape. He had to stop whatever was going on with all these reptiles. Maria had said that the snakes were hypermoulting, and feared that their life cycles were seriously jeopardized.

Looking around, Burt realized that he was standing in the middle of the central chambers of a spacious medieval castle. Although the lab looked modern not much consideration had been given to safeguarding these unique creatures. Perhaps Eva and her colleagues thought that dangerous reptiles could take care of themselves. Two small windows at the top of the room were partially open, but they were very high. The voices outside the chamber died away at dusk and a heavy, sinister shadow occupied the chamber only to be interrupted by Maria's sobs.

If only Burt could climb to those windows. As Burt looked at the walls, he realized that it was not an impossibility. *Geese! He had climbed steeper mountains than this rugged wall.*

Burt really could not recollect how he climbed or descended the wall and sought help for his assistant and the captivated reptiles. All these events would have been more appropriate for a Hitchcock movie.

The Italian police investigated and found that the operation was an international conspiracy to produce the most poisonous venom in the world, for any nation bent on using chemical warfare. Burt was there only to record this transformation of the snakes into highly poisonous ones during this three-day trial. And Eva, it had turned out, was evil.

"When are we leaving for the airport?" Maria asked in her soft voice.

"We have to hurry. Do not forget to pack my Dale Carnegie self-study book," Burt replied. This time he was going to see the blue grotto through Maria's loving eyes.

CB

Overqualified Immigrants

Many of us claim to be aware of immigration policies and the impact of mass immigration on the North American lifestyle. Yet how many of us know that for the past ten years, we've had a surplus of highly educated immigrants?

Our stereotypic image of an immigrant is a person who is uneducated, unable to understand or speak English, and has difficulty in adopting mainstream cultural values. Well, I want to take you on a stroll of the famous Robson Street in Vancouver, B.C. Robson Street is the heartbeat of the expensive tourist attractions in our beautiful city. There you will meet many different nationalities and hear many languages. This street is also very famous for different ethnic cuisines.

Are you ready for a culture shock? The typical person you see on this street is obviously of Asian, South Asian or European origin. In fact, it may be difficult to spot a true Vancouverite. The ethnic population then is clearly not a minority here. What is also striking is that all these people look busy and fairly contented.

I had the opportunity to enter the inner circles of these different looking citizens, partly because I am an immigrant myself, and secondly because in my job, I came across many troubled new immigrant families.

I made a shocking discovery on a dark, rainy winter evening. For some reason, I was the last person to leave my office building. For the first time, I came face to face with our office cleaner. He is a bald-headed, middle-aged man. He was taking his job of dusting and emptying the dustbins very seriously. He was not alone. His wife, who was dressed in an ethnic costume, was striking looking with her dark black long braid, and many gold trinkets on her. She literally tinkled whenever she dusted a table, or even took a step forwards. It was an odd couple in that the husband looked much older than the woman, who could be at the most in her late twenties.

Fully aware of my own curiosity, I managed simply to say, "Hi."

The cleaner took the opportunity to tell me that my room was the one that he enjoyed cleaning. I was slightly taken aback. Everyone knows that I am a really messy person. I wondered if he was throwing a veil of congeniality at me. I was also shocked at his very good command of English. To make my point, it will suffice to say that he enjoyed reading poems that I placed on my poem calendar everyday. I learned that he had a Master's degree from the University of Calcutta, India with English as his major.

He is not the exception to our stereotypic vision of an ill-educated immigrant. Since that encounter, I have made a conscious effort to learn the plight of highly qualified immigrants. I have met ambulance attendants and lab technicians who worked as qualified pathologists in their pre-immigration lives. I have met women who were headmistresses or teachers in their country and are now forced to take the lowest paid jobs. I have met a bus conductor who was a highly qualified biomedical engineer.

What is happening to these individuals? My friend who was a famous historian in a Polish university, but now is a real estate agent, very aptly answered this question. "Why do you think I am a real estate lady? My knowledge of world wars and ancient European history is not recognized. But history is seething in me. I have to translate my knowledge somehow. Now, I am the best real estate seller of the year. But, take a look. I am the best seller of heritage homes. No one, absolutely no one matches me, when I start my barrage of nineteenth- and early twentieth-century history. Everyone who bought houses from me bought a little piece of history and learned from me." This is indeed an example of extreme adaptability and ingenuity.

However, the other stories are not that good. Many physicians come here because of the lure of better pay and learning opportunities. Many cannot get past the qualifying exams. Most of them will eventually give up taking umpteen exams and simply take low-paid, unappreciated jobs. Take for example Jim, who was a graduate from the Chinese University of Hong Kong. He was well trained and had a dream of entering a research field. He did get some research opportunities as an assistant. After the funding was over, he was the expendable one as he did not have a long track record of working here. He was not likely to fight his case with the human rights panel. Being a proud person, he did not want to be on social assistance. He could not return to Hong Kong as his sons were well settled here in their schools. All he could do was to accept a job in a Chinese restaurant simply to survive.

There are several questions that arise from these examples. Were these highly trained persons not aware that they may not get the jobs they desired? Did someone fool them? Did they fool themselves? Are they living in a constant state of denial?

A prominent immigration lawyer tells us that there is no clear-cut answer to these questions. Some immigrants who are refugee claimants are actually in better shape and have more rights than the immigrants who enter by other legal paths. Apparently, it is not possible to control the exploitation of would-be immigrants in their country of origin. The dream of having a golden goose in a faraway country is very strong for the some. A third group of immigrants may actually be rebelling against intellectual suppression in their country of origin, and take this big leap into the unknown. Our office cleaner could fit into this category.

The government and immigration authorities are aware of this minority of highly qualified individuals. But the majority of immigrants require help with learning English, job retraining and vocational guidance. This minority of highly educated immigrants is falling between the cracks. They are highly trained intellectuals. They also have pride. It is well known that trauma to one's ego hurts more than to one's soma!

Then there is a gender paradox seen in this population. The womenfolk, even if as highly qualified as their male counterparts, easily accept the menial jobs. The males in the same category are more rigid in retraining and confronting reality. This is what I see as a gender paradox. The acculturation difficulties are expressed more severely in men, who cannot abdicate their previous positions of higher prestige. The women on the other hand make the transition along this acculturation path more easily.

There needs to be a systematic way of studying this highly

qualified mass of good citizens who would like to contribute to society but cannot. Their professional experience is said to be too much or not appropriate for a particular job. Their professional qualifications are not recognized. They would not like to go on welfare, and they won't stop dreaming.

They remind me of a story that I heard in my childhood, about a woman who spent her entire life putting together little pieces of glass and mirrors to reconstruct a broken crystal vase. In the end, she reconstructed something more beautiful than she could imagine. But it was not a vase. It was a beautiful stained window just above the altar of a church.

I do hope that each of these highly motivated individuals can make a beautiful sculpture from their fragmented dreams. I believe most of them actually succeed. Dreaming is still free and belongs to every citizen rightfully, new immigrant or native, educated or not.

Thank God for that.

CM

Rain, Rain, Go Away!

The rain was pouring down on the windshield of the 1972 multipurpose Ford Van. The old wipers were behaving erratically. Instead of flipping in two opposite directions, one of the wipers seemed to be playing "chicken" with the other. This rain was cold, harsh, and came in bucketfuls. *How was he going to make these last 15 kilometres without a mishap?*

Jake decided to pull his van to the curb and rest for a while. He had enough gas to keep it running and keep himself warm. He tried the weather channel. The prediction was for continued rain with a firm recommendation for the inhabitants not to drive in treacherous conditions. Jake became slightly uneasy.

He considered that for the first time he was really alone. All alone, though religious training came in handy. The Almighty was always there. *But I am alone,* he thought. *Rain or no rain, who can I count on?*

Perhaps your children, said a little voice in his head. *Bobby, the eldest, has no time for anybody but himself. He is 35 years old, but single and happy, married to his computers. Jackie, 24 years, definitely worries about me, but where was she when I turned 70? She'd had the dumbest excuse for not attending my anniversary. She had to care for*

15 cats in a county shelter.

"What about the poor, lonely dad?" he had asked in a joking but hurt voice. "Oh, dad! You are soooo funny!" she'd replied. "How can you compare yourself with those pooooor little darlings? They have no one…."

That is it, he thought. *I have everyone, and no one.*

He reminisced about his wife of thirty years, now deceased. Similar horrible weather witnessed her death too. It suddenly occurred to him that all the stressful events of his life were linked with heavy rainfall, storms, or some natural event beyond anyone's control.

Shirley's death on the operating table was still very vivid in his mind. Why did she have to leave him alone and vulnerable? They had taken vows never to part, and yet he was left to conquer loneliness alone. *Jeez, that is not good English. Conquering loneliness alone?*

There was no sign of the rain clearing. Even though there was no one really waiting for him, he decided to push ahead. He could visualize exactly what he could be doing when he arrived home. He would open the garage with the remote control, park his Ford inside. Then he would switch on a light at the back of the house and try to fumble with his key chain. If the rain continued pouring, he would have to use that old plastic sheet on the top of his barbecue grill to cover his head. After opening the door, he would remove his boots in the laundry room and make sure that the door was bolted well, then check the mailbox fixed to the front door. Usually, he received only bills and useless pamphlets, but he always looked at that mailbox with great anticipation. If there was no mail, he would then put on the kettle for tea.

Ugh, how monotonous is my lifestyle. Suddenly, he saw different possibilities through the rainstorm. *This rainfall is not usual and certainly not predictable and therefore this is, um, "great"?* His attempt at logical reasoning did not convince him.

He decided to be illogical. Whilst driving through the storm, he pretended that he was a messenger sent on a mission to conquer nature. He was going to continue even if it was dangerous. He had nothing to lose. And this was so much more exciting than his mundane life.

The old Ford was crackling and going ahead. He laughed as his knuckles cracked loudly, which used to be a joke between Shirley and him. *Now it is your turn, you old rickety one.* He was referring to his vehicle, of course.

There was very little movement on the road. The vehicles he passed either belonged to the foolhardy or traffic controllers. He found out the van made different sounds on water puddles at different gears. In a slow gear, the van made almost a soft, gushy sound, but if he was in the high gears going really fast, there was a sound that was very much like being at the bottom of a waterfall. It reminded him of the pleasure that he always felt in dashing through puddles.

The accompanying lightning did not deter him from his crusade. Luminous flashes were shining on water and trees. He marveled at how little a human being could do when faced with nature's games....

"Doctor, why is she not breathing? What is wrong with her, doctor? Is she gone?..." Jake with his dripping overcoat and

drenched baseball hat was almost on his knees begging the surgeons to bring Shirley to life. But Shirley was gone, just like the lightning.

At that moment, how Jake had longed to have his children. But that was not to be. They could not make it because the small airplanes could not land through the rainstorm. Loneliness, being alone, isolated, helpless, demoralized, destitute, he could think of half a dozen adjectives that could have described him for the next four months. He wondered how he had lived through this emotional storm inside him. What saved him really?

His family and friends for sure. Even Mrs. Campbell, his next door neighbour who never held his gardening skills in high esteem, offered to trim his hedges, just in case he did not feel like doing that!

Bright sunlit mornings helped. Jackie's long, frequent phone calls helped. Even Bobby's computer lessons on the internet and e-mailing rekindled something between them.

Long ago, Jake used to be interested in fishing. One day, whilst fishing on a remote lake, when he was just about to catch his trout a native elder asked him to let go of the fish. Of course, Jake was not pleased. The trout took advantage of the confusion and struggled itself free. At first, he thought that the native fisherman might have assumed that he was fishing without a proper permit, so he took that crumpled paper from his pockets.

"No, no," said the elder. "You do not understand. You have to let fish face nature. You never bargain for any living thing with nature's forces."

"What on earth....?"

Jake could not complete his sentence. A storm very similar to what he was experiencing suddenly gathered its forces. All they could do was take refuge in the little fishing shack. The storm roared for almost two hours. In that wet, cold shack, the elder's presence was even more suppressing. Jake tried to talk to him, but the man asked him to keep quiet, as if he was communicating with the storm.

After an hour or so, Jake could not bear the silence. He remembered starting to whistle, out of nervousness.

"Shhh.... Keep quiet." Listen, Mother Nature is angry."

Fifteen minutes passed and suddenly it was Jake's turn to listen to this elder. He introduced himself as "One who rides on the moon waves". He told Jake that Man was making a big mistake thinking nature could be conquered. His parting sentence was that there was only one thing that could conquer anything in the world, and that was within every living thing. He said that death could not destroy it, and it could grow phenomenally if tended.

Jake thought of the elder today. The anger of Mother Nature must have revived those sad memories of losses. The old Ford had made it home. Jake opened the garage with his remote control. As planned, he looked for the plastic sheet to cover his head, but he could not find it. The garage was quite dark, and he realized that there was no electricity. Jake found his torch. With the lit torch in his hand, he saw a heap of something on the plastic sheet, huddled with old coats and sweaters. The heap was moving and mewing.

He could not believe his eyes. Under that heap were five cats, quite shocked, with furry tails up in the air, barely mewing and returning his gaze with fluorescent glances!

What is it? He thought about Jackie. Is she all right? It was not like her to leave her "poor darlings" in the garage on the rainy day. *Oh, Almighty, help me. I do not want anything to happen to her.*

He touched the little heap. His heart was instantly filled with pity for these five little cats. His touch must have said volumes because now he could hear their crying, mewing and hissing as if the little lost babies had suddenly found their saviour.

"OK, OK, don't worry. Dad is here," Jake replied to the feline protests.

It took at least an hour to settle all of them. Out of habit, he put his hand in the mailbox, and there was a note written by Jackie on a cancelled cheque. The note read:

Dear Dad,
I had to leave Missy, Pretty, Jane, Sally and little Marisa on your doorstep. I could not find the key.... I have to go as I have an important interview and the weather forecast says that it is going to be a bad storm. The darlings will be OK and I have one tin of cat food. Love, Jackie.

It was almost ten o'clock the next day when Jackie arrived. She peered through half opened curtains. What a sight! The old fireplace was still blazing, throwing flashes on Jake's silver hairline, Missy's ears, Jane's tail and Sally's small paws. It was just like a Christmas picture postcard. All her darlings fast asleep around her dad. She had never seen her father smiling in sleep.

Jackie did not know, but her father had conquered his loneliness. He had understood what the elder had meant when he said that there was one thing that could control all atrocities of nature and that was within each living organism. Yes, he had found the key to survival through these rainstorms, calamities and feelings of doom. He would not be like a torrential rain, coming with force and wiping out everything in its way. He was well above that. He was surrounded by love, longing and life! All these forces were within him and he planned to use them.

She remembered how she used to ask rain to go away by singing, "Rain, rain go away, little Jackie wants to play." As she opened the unlocked backdoor, she softly sang to herself, "Rain, rain, you have gone away!"

ೞ

Unmathematical Equation

A little girl is very busy. She can hardly be six years of age. However, her facial expression is suggestive of a mixture of Edisonian focused attention, and a very serious intellectual look.

"Oh Mom, Mom, come quickly." Then a pregnant pause followed by a very sad sob!

"What is the matter, dear?" her mother responds

"Mom—" half the words are now swallowed by the sobs — "Mom, I did everything for this birdie. Look, I gave it water, and put cotton wool around, and tissue." More sobs and open tears now.

The birdie is dead. This is probably the first time this little girl has witnessed life extinguishing. She has worked hard on this creature. She nurtured the wounded bird with love, care, compassion, including sharing her most valuable possession, a peacock feather. Nothing had worked.

That little girl was me, a long time ago. I can still hear the conversation with my mom.

"I know you worked really hard, dear. I want you to remember one thing, though. That in caring for and loving someone, one plus one never adds to two."

A simple statement, would you say? Perhaps, but I am absolutely convinced that this is the essence of the parenting game. One plus one adds to much more than two, and it is almost impossible to subtract it to zero.

Many years later, I had the opportunity to test this wise advice. I was the parent and about to face my biggest parenting challenge up to that point. My son had thrown a huge temper tantrum over not being invited to a friend's birthday party. What does one say to a six-year-old who has already bought a present for his friend? He wanted to attend the party even though he had not been invited. His determination would have put the greatest social reformers to shame. The problem was further complicated because he could see from our front window his other friends at this party.

I was angry and very sad. These were two buddies who played together all the time. For some mysterious reason, my son had not been invited. Could it be his skin colour? It certainly had not barred two young spirits from connecting any other time.

In the flash of the moment, I made a decision: Yes, I will let my son attend the party and see what happens. I cannot describe how much courage that took, to fend for my son and relieve his despair. Yet I was not alone; a little voice was my guide, saying, "Life is not a mathematical equation, dear. One plus one never really adds to two when we care or love someone." My mother's voice! A true, true story. Yes, I could risk being a social outcast, a rebel, and yet be a foolish loving mother.

At the end of that day, one plus one added to countless invisible bonds between my son and myself. Thank you, Mom.

ଓ

Pratibha Reebye is a medical doctor who loves to write. Although more known for scientific contributions, she has always been interested in artistic pursuits. She has lived in three continents and now lives in Vancouver, Canada.

Thank you to Dania Sheldon (*left*), who edited the book, and Joyce Vandergriend (*right*) who created the cover artwork.

Printed in the United States
150783LV00012B/219/A

9 781412 091428